The Fairy Tale of
the Green Snake and
the Beautiful Lily

The Fairy Tale of
the Green Snake and
the Beautiful Lily

Johann Wolfgang von Goethe

Illustrated by

DAVID NEWBATT

Wynstones Press

Published by

Wynstones Press

Ruskin Glass Centre
Wollaston Road
Stourbridge
West Midlands DY8 4HE
England

First Edition: 2006

British Library CIP Data available.

ISBN 0 946206 58 9

Printed by Kristianstad Book Printers, Sweden.

Preface

This book has been inspired out of a wish to reset and illustrate the original Thomas Carlyle translation of this 'precious' fairy tale by Goethe, to reveal a seven-fold process that unfolds itself within the story.

I was inspired to work on this project following the research done by Paul Marshall Allen and Joan Deris Allen, found in their book 'The Time Is at Hand!' They explain in their book how Goethe's Fairy Tale of the Green Snake and the Beautiful Lily was inspired by the early seventeenth century Rosicrucian work writen by Johann Valentin Andreae, called the Chymical Wedding of Christian Rosenkreutz. This story of the Chymical Wedding depicts a journey of inner development and initiation over seven days, each day having its own special mood, threshold and challenges.

I have attempted to illustrate Goethe's Fairy Tale in seven pictures, expressing a different quality in each new time of day, from Midnight in the opening scene, to Dawn, then to Midday and onto Evening, Midnight, the following Morning and finishing with the Bright Noon-day. I have attempted to give an impression of the 'geography' of the story and the progression of events that unfolds within it.

My love of this fairy tale goes back many years and has accompanied me through all my years of working in communities of children and adults with special needs. Many times I have been involved in either acting in or producing the fairy tale as a play, and subsequently I have a deep appreciation of how living with this beautiful piece of writing can have a profound effect on ones personal development and relationship to others in life.

David Newbatt 2006.

The Green Snake and the Beautiful Lily

Introduction by Tom Raines

"The Goethe fairy tale is a marvellous work, one must live it, not merely read it."

Rudolf Steiner

A true fairy story is a work of art. At Michaelmas, in 1795, there appeared in the German magazine D*ie Horen* (The Hours) a series of stories of which the concluding one was A F*airy Tale of T*he Green Snake and the Beautiful Lily. This tale tells of magical transformation, yet one which, when the time is ripe, can be experienced by every human being. The author of these stories was Johann Wolfgang von Goethe and the creation of this Fairy Tale was to have far reaching consequences. Who was this man and what was the significance of his Fairy Tale?

This introduction to the Fairy Tale and its creator, brief though it is – for one could surely write a whole book and still leave much unsaid – offers the reader a broad sketch of Goethe's life as it unfolded up until the moment he committed his tale to the written word. This gives us some ground upon which to stand as we look together at how the Fairy Tale came to be created, following a little of its destiny in the world and seeking what might be its relevance for us in our time.

Goethe entered the world on August 28th, 1749 in Frankfurt am Main, Germany. He was destined to become a giant in the cultural life of Europe, producing a truly astounding body of work during the course of his 82 years of life on earth. Goethe's contribution to world literature is universally acknowledged, the breadth and depth of which in its wisdom has often been termed 'Olympian'.

His creative work and interests encompassed many areas and disciplines, including those of critic, journalist, painter, theatre manager, educationalist and natural philosopher. He produced prose and poetry across a variety of themes, displaying a command of many styles, whilst never losing the power to produce magical, short lyrics wherein he made the manifold mystery of human existence transparent. His creative faculties remained remarkably intact to the end of his life, epitomised by his masterpiece, F*aust*, that he worked on and developed for 60 years, completing it just before his death on 23rd March, 1832.

Goethe was also a natural scientist and his writings in this field alone produced some 14 volumes. He recognised that in observing natural processes, like a growing plant, a large part of the process of such a living organism's 'coming into being' is invisible to our normal senses. A contemporary of Goethe's, born some six years before him, was the philosopher Kant, whose ideas still stand behind much of our modern thinking. It was Kant who stated that the type of intelligence necessary to know these hidden processes in organic nature would be an intuitive intellect – *intellectus archetypus* – that, Kant asserted, was beyond the capacity of humankind. Nature, when revealed, manifests both the truth of scientific knowledge and the beauty of the creative act. But these were separate for Kant: Science was separated from Art. Goethe, however, brought art into his approach to science and made of them a unity. He did an enormous research work on how to observe Nature and in so doing brought a new approach to natural science. He was both a student and a 'revealer' in artistic form, of the secrets of inner human nature and the outer manifestations of Mother Nature. His own experiences showed him that through a willingness to observe with the senses, free of any preconceptions, deepening this process to the point of becoming aware of one's inner responses, then one could come to an intuitive knowing of Nature's hidden processes. He held the conviction that both art and science led to, and sprang from, the 'primal source of all being' out of which came the whole of creation. His Fairy Tale belongs to this source.

Born into a middle-class family of cultured parents, Goethe received a wide and rich education. His father was a retired lawyer from the North of Germany. His mother, the daughter of a Mayor of Frankfurt, was able, in time, to open up many connections for her son with the dignitaries of that city. At the age of 17, Goethe would have preferred to have read classics at the then newly founded University of Gottingen where the influence of English prevailed, but instead, he followed in his father's footsteps for a moment by going to study law at the University of Leipzig.

A few years later, in July 1768, he awoke one night in a desperate state; his lungs were haemorrhaging. He suffered an enormous loss of blood and nearly died. A long period of recuperation followed and for the next two years he was cared for at his Frankfurt home by Susanna Katarina von Klettenberg, a friend and distant relative of his mother.

Susanna von Klettenberg was a mystic with deep spiritual perception and was a member of the *Herrenhuter*, the Moravian Church. This was a religious movement having its roots in the 15th Century *Unitas Fratrum* (*Unity of Brethren or Brothers*) Hussite movement of Bohemia and Moravia. This woman had realised that this near death experience was a turning point in the young Goethe's life. As well as caring for his physical needs, she guided him into an awareness of spiritual realms of which he had been previously unaware. She brought him into contact with many written works on mystical subjects, especially books on alchemy by such men as Paracelsus, Basilius Valentinus and Franciscus Mercurius van Helmont. She had a friend, also a member of the *Herrenhuter*, a physician and alchemist called Dr. Johann Freidrich Metz, under whose care and unique medicinal remedies Goethe slowly recovered. The deeper background of alchemy is connected to the Rosicrucians, those people who serve the aims of the individuality known as Christian Rosenkreutz, who seeks to further the work of The Christ by transforming and spiritualising the Human Soul and the Earth. Through his life-threatening illness, Goethe was brought into connection with the knowledge of the Rosicrucians and out of this influence and inspiration he was eventually to create his Fairy Tale.

Following his recuperation, Goethe transferred his studies to the University of Strasbourg where he developed a deep interest in natural science, history and folklore. He was now very active with his poetry and from this period came some of his finest lyric poems. Susanna von Klettenberg died in 1774 and Goethe was to later write a moving tribute to her *Bekenntnisse einer schonen Seele* (*The Confessions of a Beautiful Soul*) that he included in his novel *Wilhelm Meister*. That same year, Goethe had a meeting in Frankfurt with Karl August, Duke of Sachse-Weimar, a man who was to play a great role in his life. Eight years younger than Goethe, Karl August invited him to come to the city of Weimar and act as his personal advisor and counsellor. Initially Goethe agreed to come for only a few months, but this was to become his home for the rest of his life. Here Goethe took up ever-increasing responsibilities on behalf of the Duke and the affairs of State. This often involved extensive correspondence, interviews, conferences, travel and social obligations. One of the duties he was called upon to perform was that of inspector of mines and this took him to Illmenau, a few miles away from Weimar. Here, he became deeply interested in geology and mining principles. Through this work, coupled with the fact that Goethe's official residence was a *Gartenhaus* (*Garden House*) in a park on the edge of Weimar, we can perhaps see how this man's lively interest would be stimulated by the abundant plant and mineral forms with which he was coming more and more into contact. This interest would have been further supported by the proximity of the Thuringian forests and the herbalists he would often meet in the woodland countryside. Yet, all these duties were placing an increasing burden on Goethe, leaving less and less time for his own creative work, for he was now also director of the Weimar Theatre and was expected to write new plays as well as supervise stage productions. Finally, desperate for a release, he slipped quietly away for an extended visit to Italy in 1786. This was to last for over two years.

This journey to Italy had a profound effect on Goethe. The architecture, sculptings and paintings he discovered, influenced by the Greek, Roman and Italian cultures, drew forth many deep observations and insights from his soul. In the diary Goethe kept of this journey, he made the following entry under 6th September 1787: ". . . Supreme works of art, like the most sublime products of Nature, are created by man in conformity with true and natural law. All that is arbitrary, all that is invented, collapses: there is Necessity, there is God." Goethe began to observe nature in a new and creative way. His faculty of observation, of 'seeing' ever more deeply into natural phenomena, was unfolding more and more and Nature began to reveal her secrets to him. In the botanical garden at Padua, whilst looking at a 'Fan' Palm tree, Goethe realised the importance of the *leaf-form*, showing itself in various stages of metamorphosis in a plant. This discovery worked further in Goethe, until, later in his journey, when he was in Sicily visiting the botanical garden of Palermo, it culminated in his receiving the profound experience of 'seeing' with his inner eye the '*Urpflanze*' – the 'archetypal plant' – the creative form behind all plant life. A new approach to science was now developing within Goethe, whereby he observed not only what was the phenomenon before him, but also what inner activity was called forth in him in those moments. Goethe conceived science as a path of inner development, where, by means of intensifying the sensory observation, the inner faculties of imagination, inspiration and intuition could come alive, enabling one to break through to a spiritual understanding of what was at the very root and heart of the natural world and its manifold manifestations. He felt that science should have as its highest goal the arousal of wonder through contemplative observation in which the scientist would come to see "God in Nature and Nature in God". Goethe wanted to open the eyes of the observer to what was spiritually at work in nature. His was a voice speaking over two hundred years ago, and yet his approach seems pressingly relevant today. It could be argued that the ecological crisis facing the modern world is really a crisis of our *relationship* to nature. The problem we face is not the degradation of nature, but rather the degradation of our *awareness* of nature. Many people today do not know how to look more deeply into nature for themselves, feeling that this must be the preserve of scientific 'experts', yet Goethe saw the human being as "the most powerful and exact instrument if we but take the trouble sufficiently to refine our sensibilities".

The events, the artistic and natural impressions which gave rise to so many insights during his Italian Journey, Goethe recreated as a book, the reading of which clearly reveals how some of the experiences he made in Italy later became metamorphosed into aspects of his Fairy Tale. Goethe's scientific approach to observing nature is one that can also be applied to the reading of his Fairy Tale. If we recreate his word pictures in our imagination, we can observe them with the 'inner eye' and allow what they may reveal to speak to us.

On his return to Weimar, a loneliness descended upon Goethe as he discovered that few understood his newly awakened scientific awareness, preferring to admire only his poems and written stories. Nevertheless, he chose to plunge deeper into his scientific studies. These efforts bore an early fruit with the publication in 1790 of the *Metamorphosis of the Plant*. Here, Goethe followed the plant through archetypal stages of alternating expansion and contraction. He saw the leaf as the constant underlying form in the plant that was metamorphosed forwards and backwards (if we imagine the leaf as central in the plant between root/stem and flower), appearing in different forms as root, stem, leaf, bud, flower and fruit, or seed. He followed this a year later with the publication of his first essay on optics, which led to his monumental study of colour phenomena, *Zur Farbenlehre* (*Theory of Colour*, eventually published in 1810). Here, Goethe challenged the theories of Newton that sought to explain the phenomenon of colour in terms of the measurable angles of refrangibility of colourless rays of light, thus reducing the phenomenon of colour to a dead mechanism. Goethe's approach was to try and understand colour in its own terms as he experienced it arising out of the meeting of light and darkness in nature. He saw colour as the "deeds and sufferings of light" as it manifested itself on the material plane. He treated it as something living. It is a qualitative approach that has always appealed more to artists than to scientists. J. W. Turner, the English artist and contemporary of Goethe, experimented at the end of his life with Goethe's theories and in the process painted some masterpieces.

Goethe came to recognise three principles at work in organic nature: metamorphosis, polarity and enhancement. In other words: changing of form, the meeting of opposites (for example, day and night) and a climax or 'crowning glory' in a piece of creation (like a flower on top of a plant). It is just these qualities of magical change, meeting of opposites and glorious moments of achievement, of fulfilment, that one finds in a Fairy Tale! When we bear this in mind, Goethe's life-path of development as a natural scientist – bringing his art into science and his science into art – becomes more visibly relevant to his ability to create a true Fairy Tale.

We have touched upon two occasions in Goethe's life when inner soul changes occurred, signalled by outer circumstances. Around the age of 18 he had a life-threatening illness and was led to a spiritual perspective of life through a person deeply connected to the Rosicrucian stream. Around the age of 37 he took an extended journey to Italy and deepened his faculty of observation, beginning to see Nature more with his 'inner eye'. Art and a new science open out for Goethe. These were times in his life when something happened which shaped his destiny, when he was able to take hold of new forces on his life's path. These moments occurred around the 'lunar node' periods of Goethe's life. What is this cosmic measure, the lunar node?

Briefly, viewed from the Earth, the orbits of the Sun and Moon are inclined at an angle to one another and intersect in two places. When the Moon is physically at one of these two intersecting points, and at the same moment is in a straight line with the Earth and Sun, this is called a lunar node. This special alignment occurs approximately every 19 years (18 years, 7 months, 11 days to be more exact). When a person is born, their body, soul and spirit unite on the earth. Ancient wisdom connected Earth, Moon and Sun with body, soul and spirit and so a person's birth was understood as a moment when the different aspects of these three heavenly bodies were in a spiritual 'alignment.' Of course the physical astronomical alignment does not occur with each person's birth, but its recurring *rhythm* of approximately 19 years was seen as applicable to every human birth, repeating itself throughout a person's life. The moment of birth is the moment we take up the journey of our earthly destiny, and the occurrence through our life of our lunar nodes can be seen as moments that can reveal something of our destiny in a special way, when seemingly outer events appear to shape something of our lives. For Goethe, the first repeat of his lunar node came at the time of his illness and the second occurred during his Italian journey. Occult knowledge of the stars offers the picture that around each time the rhythm of the lunar node occurs in a person's life, something of their true earthly destiny shines strongly into their life, illuminating and quickening it. This seems unmistakable in Goethe's life.

In the spring of 1794, Goethe travelled to listen to a lecture in Jena and afterwards, on the steps outside the building where the lecture had been given, he shared with the philosopher Schiller his experience of the archetypal plant. Schiller responded to Goethe's words by saying "That is not a description of something objective, but is only an idea." To this Goethe replied "Then it is clear that I see my *ideas* with my eyes." This conversation was to mark the beginning of a wonderful and fruitful friendship, where both found enormous stimulation through each other's ideas. This relationship surely helped to alleviate the sense of loneliness that Goethe felt, for in Schiller he had found a kindred spirit with whom he could share his natural-scientific ideas.

Later that year Schiller proposed the publishing of a literary periodical to be called *Die Horen* and asked Goethe if he would like to contribute. Goethe was enthusiastic and as his first contribution offered a series of stories grouped together under the title *Unterhaltungen deutscher Ausgewanderteen* (*Conversations with German Emigrants*).

These stories grew as a response to the times in which they were written. Goethe was born and raised during the period when the French movement of 'Enlightenment' brought rationalism strongly into European thinking. This one-sided intellectual thinking was a ferment for the subsequent French Revolution at the end of the 18th Century. It is clear that Goethe was no rationalist and the waves breaking over his soul at this time as a consequence of events stemming from this way of thinking became a deep burden for him. Two years before, Louis XVI, the King of France, had been executed and now in 1794 the revolution was at its height and thousands of refugees were fleeing for their lives before the armies of France. Goethe took these events as the background for his series of stories for *Die Horen*. In them he had a group of dispossessed and exiled aristocrats wondering and fearing about the future. They represented, in their various characters, something of a cross section of humanity. Tensions built up between them and in order to help maintain a peaceful existence together it was suggested that, taking it in turns, on each evening one person should tell a story to the group, to give a little common ground to their small community and help raise their spirits. And so Goethe weaves six tales. Finally an old clergyman in the group proposes he relates the seventh and last tale to be told, which will be a Fairy Tale. He says, quite enigmatically, that it will remind them of "everything and nothing." Through the character of the old clergyman Goethe introduces *The Fairy Tale of the Green Snake and the Beautiful Lily*. In *the context of the Conversations with German Emigrants* it is totally different in style and content to the proceeding six tales and clearly stands as a tale by itself.

This Fairy Tale was written by Goethe as a response to a work of Schiller's entitled *Über die aesthetische Erziehung des Menschen* (*Letters on the Aesthetic Education of Man*). One of the main thoughts considered in these 'letters' centred around the question of human freedom. What should be the condition of the human soul forces to achieve this freedom? Schiller recognised Necessity (instinct, passion, the realm of the Senses) and Reason as two forces in the human soul. If either one predominated over the other, it prevented the human being from attaining real freedom; either the soul would be driven by blind necessity, or else a cold reason would suppress all passion and instinct. Only by establishing a middle ground, where necessity and reason harmonised, could freedom exist. Thus Schiller had conceived of a threefold model of the human being, where, in the balance between the two poles of Necessity and Reason, Freedom would exist for the Human Personality. Schiller saw that a harmonious social life could only be founded on the basis of free human personalities. He saw that there was an 'ideal human being' within everyone and the challenge was to bring the outer life experiences into harmony with this 'ideal.' Then the human being would lead a truly worthy existence. Schiller was trying to build an inner bridge between the person in the immediate reality and the 'ideal human being.' He wrote these 'Letters' during the time and context of the French Revolution. This revolution was driven by a desire for *outer* social changes to enable human personalities to become free. But both Schiller and Goethe recognised that freedom cannot be 'imposed' from the outside but must arise from *within* each person. Whilst he had an artistic nature, Schiller was more at home in the realm of philosophic thoughts and although Goethe found much pleasure in these 'Letters' of Schiller, he felt that the approach concerning the forces in the soul was too simply stated and, it should be said, working in abstract ideas was not Goethe's way. So he set about writing a Fairy Tale that would show, in imaginative pictures, the way in which a human soul could become whole and free, thereby giving rise to a new and free human community, and this was published in *Die Horen* in 1795. Goethe's life continued, encompassing many notable experiences and achievements but we will let his biography rest here, for we have arrived at the moment of birth of *The Green Snake and the Beautiful Lily* through his creative hands.

Goethe lived in a moment of history that carried profound inspirations on its breath. Between the Rationalist period of European thinking and the beginning of scientific materialism around the third decade of the nineteenth century (about the time of Goethe's death), there happened a most creative period of human thinking and consciousness. This was the moment known as the Classical period in Germany that was followed by a brief flowering of Romanticism all over Europe through such people as William Blake in England, with his prophetic art and poetry, and Novalis in Germany who brought through his poetry and other writings a spiritual interpretation of Cosmos, Humanity and Earth. Goethe was perhaps the most prominent representative of this movement, who, with his contemporaries, stood in the world for a moment, united by their endeavours to open a new thinking for a new knowledge, vouchsafing the future development of humanity. When this wave of spiritual endeavour receded under the pressure of scientific materialism, its achievements looked to a future time for a deeper unfolding. Are we now ripe for this in the 21st Century? Could we say for ourselves, "The Time has Come?"

This cry, "The Time has Come!" rings throughout Goethe's Fairy Tale, which is set in a landscape divided by a river. This acts as a boundary between two lands, that of our normal 'daytime' consciousness and that which is not accessible to our normal sense perception - The Land of the Senses and the Land of the Spirit. By the end of the Fairy Tale, there is a permanent bridge spanning this river, joining these two Lands together. The theme of love and sacrifice bringing about a true and harmonious community emerges as the tale unfolds. Many magical and seemingly illogical happenings occur, as is the way with any true fairy tale because they have their own laws at work within them. These are not understandable through the rationale of our normal intellectual logic, rather it is a higher spiritual 'logic' that is at work. Goethe's understanding of the three principles in nature of metamorphosis, polarity and enhancement – or moment of climax – do not seem out of place in approaching this 'higher logic'. A number of different characters appear in his Fairy Tale, interacting with one another, weaving together towards a climax that is experienced with the marriage between the Beautiful Lily and her Prince and the joining together, by means of the bridge, of the two Lands. The one event is dependent and linked to the other.

The Fairy Tale begins with a Ferryman, asleep, who lives in a small hut by the river. It is midnight and he is woken up by two Will-o'-wisps – gentlemen seemingly made of flames of light – and asked to take them across the river. This he does. But the Ferryman can only take passengers in this direction, none can return with him from the other side. Later, we realise that they are crossing over from the land of the Spirit to the land of the Senses. Soon there is a meeting with a Green Snake. She lives in a chasm in the rocks and has access to an underground chamber which is later revealed to be a temple containing four Kings; one each of Gold, Silver, Bronze and the fourth a mixture of all three. The Will-o'-wisps devour gold wherever they find it, licking it up with their flames of light, then later shaking gold coins from themselves. By eating the gold coins shaken from the Will-o'-wisps, the Green Snake is able to shine a light from within herself which illuminates her surroundings. It is in the underground Temple of the Kings that we first meet the Old Man with the Lamp. His is a special lamp that can only give light when another light is already present. It is he who first speaks the words, "The Time has Come!", upon hearing a secret whispered into his ear by the Snake. The tale moves on and we meet the Wife of the Old Man with the Lamp. She leads the story further when she meets a young Prince walking in melancholy mood by the river. He loves the Beautiful Lily, but cannot approach her because, lovely though she is, her touch brings death to all living things, a fate which is deeply distressing to her as well as the Prince. So now we learn the central sorrow and tension of the tale. How will this be overcome?

There are moments at Midday, Midnight, Twilight and Dawn when the river can be crossed the other way, back from the sense-perceptible land to the Spirit Land. At Midday and Midnight the Green Snake transforms her body into a temporary bridge across the river whereas the shadow of a Giant performs the same function at Twilight and Dawn. Through this we are shown that there are two possible ways to cross the river from the Land of the Senses, but only at these special times. The scenes follow one another from midnight to dawn, through midday to twilight and a second midnight, dawn and finally midday when all is resolved. Seven stages, that most rhythmical of numbers. By crossing the temporary bridge formed by the Green Snake at Midday, the Wife and the young Prince come to the garden of the Beautiful Lily. In this garden, attended by her three handmaidens, we witness the Beautiful Lily sorrowing for her own condition yet bringing joy, wonder and love to all who meet with her. At Twilight, when the rich colours of the day gradually die into the night, tragedy befalls the Prince, who, overcome by his desire for the Beautiful Lily, rushes towards her and his life is extinguished by her touch. The Green Snake, who is also present, immediately forms a circle around the Prince, clenching her tail between her teeth. The Old Man with the Lamp reappears as does his Wife and the Will-o'-wisps. Under the guidance of the Man with the Lamp the whole group crosses over the bridge, formed by the Snake at Midnight, back into the Land of the Senses. Here remarkable transformations occur. Guided by the Old Man, the Beautiful Lily touches the Snake with her left hand and the Prince with her right, whereby he is brought back to life, but in a dream-like state. The Green Snake changes herself into a pile of precious gems that are then thrown into the river. With the help of the Will-o'-wisps' ability to eat gold, the group re-enters the underground Temple of the Kings. This Temple now magically moves beneath the river, coming up underneath the Ferryman's hut, which falls into the open roof of the temple and is transformed into a beautiful silver altar inside the Temple. The Whole Temple has now arisen from the Earth and stands in the sunlight. The Three Kings of Gold, Silver and Bronze bestow gifts on the Prince that together overcome his dream-like state, restoring his full consciousness and stature. The fourth, 'mixed metal' King has had his gold 'veins' licked away by the Will-o'-wisps and has collapsed. The Prince can now be united in marriage with the Beautiful Lily, for her touch no longer brings death. As King and Queen they look out from the Temple and see that a *permanent* Bridge now spans the river across which people are travelling to and fro. This Bridge is the result of the sacrifice of the Green Snake, cast as precious stones into the river. Now the two lands are united for all humanity and the final words of the Fairy Tale tell us ". . . the Bridge, to this day, is swarming with travellers and the Temple is the most frequented in the whole world."

It is not the purpose of this article to retell the whole story with all its wonderful details, but to look only at a few themes and events that may help to bring alive its relevance for us. Many seemingly small details in this tale hold a world of knowledge and wisdom within them and it is the contemplation of this tale and all it contains which can lead to new and deeper understanding of some of the mysteries of the human soul.

So, finally, we follow a little more of the destiny of this Fairy Tale, for it brings us to a man who, more than any other, has helped reveal the spiritual wealth contained within it.

In February, 1882, on the occasion of his 21st birthday, Rudolf Steiner (who would later found the spiritual movement of Anthroposophy) received a copy of *The Green Snake and the Beautiful Lily*. It was given to him by Karl Julius Schroer, whom Steiner referred to as his "teacher and fatherly friend". Steiner read the tale with interest but could not yet penetrate its deeper meanings, although he returned to it a number of times in the years to come. It lay in Steiner's destiny, after gaining his doctorate at university, to be invited to go to Weimar to edit Goethe's writings on Natural Science. Whilst there, the inner depth of the Fairy Tale began to reveal itself to him. Later, he was to describe how "it was in the late eighties of the last century that the knot of Goethe's Fairy Tale untied itself for me" and that by understanding how Goethe had arranged the sequence of pictures in the tale, Steiner realised they made possible a transforming power on the soul of the reader. He felt moved to make the profound statement: "this is the new way to Christ." A great work of art only reveals itself in its deeper Being to one who is patient, allowing time, not forcing an understanding. This was to be Steiner's experience. On November 27th, 1891, Steiner spoke about "The Secret in Goethe's Fairy Tale" at the Goethe Society in Vienna. He later recalled that the Fairy Tale came strongly once more into his inner life in 1896. In the years that followed, according to Steiner's own biography, he went through a tremendous inner struggle with the materialism of the age in which he lived, culminating in him "standing in the spiritual presence of the Mystery of Golgotha in a most profound and solemn festival of knowledge". Shortly after this experience, in 1899, Steiner, now 38 years old, wrote an essay to commemorate the 150th anniversary of Goethe's birth, entitled *The Character of Goethe's Spirit as Shown in the Fairy Tale of the Green Snake and the Beautiful Lily*, which was published in Berlin in "The Magazine for Literature" during August of that year. A year later, at Michaelmas, September 29th, 1900, Steiner gave a private lecture where he spoke about the Fairy Tale under the title *Goethe's Secret Revelation (Goethe's geheime Offenbarung)*. He was later to refer to this as his first anthroposophical lecture. Throughout his life he made mention on many occasions concerning this Fairy Tale. Of course, there were many other influences at work in Steiner's life, but the significance of his relationship to Goethe, his work and particularly the Fairy Tale cannot be overlooked. It is in acknowledging Steiner's insights to this tale that we now return for a look at some of its themes, but perhaps bearing in mind what he said of his own approach to understanding the Fairy Tale, "I did not write a commentary, I let the living lead me into the living."

The theme of Goethe's Fairy Tale is the transformation of the soul, which is an alchemical process. The Fairy Tale itself is a piece of alchemy, as Steiner discovered, whereby he was able to state from his own spiritual research that it was a work of art inspired by Rosicrucian wisdom. We may recall that with his illness around the age of 18, Goethe was led into connection with spiritual writings particularly those concerning alchemy. Goethe read, a number of times, a work entitled *The Chymical Wedding of Christian Rosenkreutz: Anno 1459* which was first published in Strasbourg in 1616. This book contained, in pictorial imaginations, the experience of an initiation in the spiritual worlds. Those serving the Rosicrucian path are concerned with the transformation of substance – both the substance of the human soul and of the earth Herself. Matter can be viewed as condensed spirit, darkened light, held fast, 'spellbound,' enchanted into physical form, as it were. When a transforming spiritual impulse can penetrate into matter, the condensed, imprisoned spirit-form can be released anew into pure spirit. The transforming of 'soul substance' is the overcoming of selfish human desires, making the soul a fit vessel for the spirit. Spiritual transformation of substance is the basis of a true alchemy. Goethe's Fairy Tale has an inner architecture that follows alchemical principles. These principles – of separation, purification and re-combining in a new way – can be seen in the tale: the differentiation of the characters and their tasks, the purification through love and sacrifice (which the Green Snake willingly does), then leading to a new community life-condition imbued with spirit. On the way through this process, death occurs, showing the Rosicrucian principle of 'dying in order to become.' This principle Goethe upheld in his own life and creative work. Nature, going through Her cycles, readily describes this process with the dying away in autumn and the birth of new life in spring.

Schiller's conceptual thoughts concerning human freedom and the soul forces of the human being became, through Goethe's imaginative creativity, the figures and events in his Fairy Tale. He allowed his imaginative pictures to grow and metamorphose towards the solution to the question of how the human soul attains to freedom. Steiner maintained that the various figures in the Fairy Tale were supersensibly perceived in Goethe's imagination and therefore are true to themselves – not born from flights of fancy, but coming from the realm of real Imagination, through Goethe, as artistic phantasy. The Beautiful Lily is a picture of the pure spiritual forces, the embodiment of Freedom not accessible to the soul in its normal state, thus the river separating the 'two lands', the one of the spirit where the Beautiful Lily lives and the one of the senses, where the young Prince lives. Unprepared souls die at her touch. This indicates that a soul must be ripe in its powers to be able to *consciously* receive the spirit into it. The Green Snake, who has her home in a cleft in the rocks, is the embodiment of the subter-ranean forces of the soul. Life on Earth brings experiences to the human soul, and the Green Snake is the embodiment of the sum of these experiences which when ripe, when 'the Time has come', can be sacrificed to form a permanent and fully conscious bridge to the spirit. These two conditions – of Lily and Snake – must be freely united in the soul in order for it to fulfil its true being. (Here we might recall Schiller's three-fold picture.) The young Prince is the seeking soul. By the end of the tale, his unity with the Beautiful Lily has come about due to the awakening of previously slumbering soul forces enabling the Prince to unite with Freedom through the sacrifice of his life experience, when the time is ripe, as embodied in the actions of the Green Snake. His earthly life experience has now been transformed, becoming a new inner quality uniting the 'two lands.' This is the new condition of soul that both Schiller and Goethe were striving to experience: The Free Human Personality. This soul transformation, bringing about new human community, is the outcome of the Fairy Tale.

The Old Man with the Lamp has an important role in the whole. He is that soul force which is the guide knowing when the *time is right* what to do. In the first Temple scene the gold King asks him about secrets. The old man says he knows three. The King then asks which is the most important. The Old Man says he will reveal that when he learns the fourth secret. At that moment the Green Snake approaches and whispers in his ear. Then the Old Man cries out "The Time has Come!" We do not learn directly in this moment what the snake has said, but, later in the tale, as she is curled around the dead Prince, she again speaks to the Old Man and tells him that she is willing to sacrifice herself. This she does. Steiner shows that what she whispered to the Old Man in the Temple was her free resolve to sacrifice herself. The Old Man knew that she must make her sacrifice, but he had to wait until she did it of her own free will. Then he could say, "The Time has Come!"

The Christian path to Love is one of Sacrifice. In the Fairy Tale it is the sacrifice of the loving Green Snake that provides the force to make all things possible. Now we may better understand the title of this Fairy Tale. The Snake and the Lily are the two poles that the striving soul must unite in the right way to gain Freedom for itself. But other forces must also play their part, and we learn that they all receive their transformations at the end of the tale.

Three times in the tale the Old man speaks out "The Time has Come!" In the Temple, a little while later to his Wife and then again in the Temple with the whole group. Three times the Beautiful Lily hears these words spoken out: by the Wife when she relates events to her, by the Green Snake who also speaks to her and finally in the presence of the Old Man in the final Temple scene. Three is a powerful number; it relates to the Holy Trinity and is always present, in some form, in a true Fairy Tale. Weaving through Goethe's tale, the three cries by the Old Man precipitate action. The three 'hearings' by the Beautiful Lily unite past, present and future into an eternal *now*. Once, twice, thrice! builds a force that must be heard. The Time has Come! This full moment of will for action is the crucible for change. New conditions then appear.

The element of three appears also with the Kings of Gold, Silver and Bronze who bestow gifts on the Prince, bringing him to a full consciousness of his new Kingdom. These three Kings are related to the soul faculties of Thinking, Feeling and Willing, or Doing, and their individual gifts strengthen these three, newly separated realms in the Prince. These realms have to become independent in order to work freely with one another within the soul. In the normal human condition they are mixed together, like the fourth King, and bring chaotic conditions into the human soul, making it unfree. This understanding of these three forces working freely in the healthy human soul enabled Steiner, later in his life, to develop a threefold picture of society. He envisaged society as composed of three independent but freely associating realms: the free spiritual-cultural life, the life of equal legal-rights between people and brotherhood in the economic life. There was a prefiguring of this in the ideals of the French revolution of Liberty, Equality and Fraternity, but they could not be realised as true social forms because they were viewed from an external perspective and not as qualities coming from the actual soul configuration of the Free Human Personality.

Gold and light also weave together as themes throughout the Fairy Tale. Gold appears both as wisdom, in the gold King, and money, in the gold coins. It shows two sides of itself in human hands, bringing illumination and wisdom or suffering. When eaten by the Green Snake it causes her to shine light, but when a little dog belonging to the Wife eats some gold coins shaken down by the Will-o'-wisps, it dies. The Old Man's Lamp, when no other light is present, turns stone into gold. It is a wise Light. In the Fairy Tale, light appears in many forms, not least as the waxing and waning of daylight which places events at different times of the day and night.

Here we could mention how the temporary bridges of the Green Snake and the Shadow of the Giant relate to the soul's relationship to the spiritual World. These are moments in the Fairy Tale when it is possible to cross over from the Land of the Senses to the Land of the Spirit. In life, art is a bridge to the spirit. In creating art and entering its phantasy, the human being can be free for a moment, in touch with the creative source of things. This is the secret of the Green Snake forming a bridge at Midday and Midnight, for this enables – just at those moments – a crossing from the Land of the Senses to the Land of the Spirit. The Shadow of the Giant at Twilight and Dawn is another matter. One can also cross the river by this means, but, as the name 'shadow' implies, it is done not in full consciousness. It happens at Twilight or Dawn when things are not so definite, it is not clearly day or night as in the Midday-Midnight moments when the Green Snake makes her temporary Bridge. And it is not the Giant who can take people across, only his shadow. There is a dimming of awareness, one which we can understand in our modern times through the experiences people have when access to spiritual experiences is found by the use of drugs, or dubious mediumistic practices and the like. These are not clear paths to the spirit, in conscious knowledge, but access is gained through a 'shadow' of this knowledge.

The reader is invited to approach this Fairy Tale and make his or her own discoveries as well as look further into the wealth of insights that Steiner brought. The tale can be seen as a picture of one human soul. All the figures and events in the tale are the interacting forces within the one, striving, human soul. But within this context the forces have an individual existence, which Goethe's characters give expression to. There are something like 20 characters in this tale. We have looked at some of the elements that exist in it as a means of orientating towards a deeper experience. Ultimately the tale itself should be allowed to reveal its own nature to each reader. Then, perhaps, a living understanding of the tale will also reveal itself, when the time has come!

The Fairy Tale went through its own metamorphosis.

Concerning the question of how the soul can attain freedom and create healthy social forms, Schiller, with his *thinking*, grasped the idea of a way forward. Goethe transformed it through phantasy into the *feeling* life of pictorial imagination. Rudolf Steiner completed this trilogy by transforming the Fairy Tale into a Mystery Drama, performed on the stage; he brought it into the *will*. In his autobiography, Steiner said the following: "The Goethe Fairy Tale images hark back to Imaginations which had often been set forth before the time of Goethe by seekers for the spiritual experience of the soul... not the interpretation, but the stimulus to the experience of the soul was the important result that came to me from my work upon the Fairy Tale. This stimulus later influenced the future life of my soul in the shaping of the mystery dramas I afterwards wrote."

Originally Steiner had intended to create a dramatic form of Goethe's Fairy Tale, but discovered that it could not happen because "it was clearly necessary to present these images in a far more concrete manner suited for our time." And so Steiner metamorphosed the figures of Goethe's Fairy Tale, essentially the different soul forces at work in one human soul, into individual human beings, where one soul force or another predominates, dealing with life's tensions in a contemporary setting. This drama he called "The Portal of Initiation." It is possible when reading both the Fairy Tale and this Mystery Drama to see which characters belong together. For example, the Green Snake has become the 'Other Maria' in Steiner's Drama, a self-sacrificing nurse. The Beautiful Lily is 'Maria' who has attained much in spiritual development and helps a man called Johannes to also develop further. In him we have Goethe's young Prince. The Old Man has become Felix Balde, a nature-mystic echoing the qualities of Jacob Boehme (a German mystic of the Middle ages). And so on. The characters in this mystery drama show the relationship of karma and destiny in human souls striving to come closer to the spirit. This Drama was performed in 1910 and Steiner wrote three more. In the second he drew upon traditions of the Knights Templar. The third and fourth Steiner claims as purely his own, representing the workings of Anthroposophy. In order to find a permanent home for the performances of these Dramas a wooden building was created in Dornach, Switzerland. This was burned down in 1923 and a second building, this time in concrete, grew out of the ashes. They both bore the name the *Goetheanum* in honour of the man who had so deeply influenced Steiner's life and had provided the artistic seed inspiration for his own

Mystery Dramas. Steiner was to say that Goethe's Fairy Tale was the archetypal seed of the Anthroposophical movement. Indeed, just as the Green Snake sacrificed herself to form the bridge which could permanently unite the 'two lands', so Steiner gave his life's work to create, through anthroposophy, a *living* bridge into the spiritual worlds from our Earthly sense-perceptible one. He realised on earth something of the 'Crowning Glory' of Goethe's Fairy Tale.

In his Mystery Dramas Steiner honoured the Fairy Tale as a form of artistic expression by having Felix Balde's wife, Felicia (the metamorphosed 'Old Man' and 'Wife' from Goethe's Fairy Tale) recite Fairy Tales she herself has created. In a lecture he gave concerning his second Mystery drama, Steiner had the following to say: "In our time there begins that new age in which it becomes necessary again to find access to higher worlds. For this a certain transition must be established and it is scarcely possible to make this transition more simply than by a sensible revival of a feeling for Fairy Tales. Between that spiritual world to which man can raise himself by clairvoyance and the world of the intellect and the senses, the Fairy Tale is perhaps the truest of all mediums. The very way in which the modest Fairy Tale approaches us, not laying claim in any sense to be an image of external reality but boldly disregarding all outer laws of external realities, makes it possible for the Fairy Tale to prepare the human soul to receive again the higher spiritual world."

There will always be new things to discover within this tale because any living story, concerned with the verities of human existence, be it called myth, legend or Fairy Tale, has the ability to grow through the ages as a companion to humanity – alive in its own right because they, like us, come out of the spirit's creative source. We may recall that, when Goethe first published the Fairy Tale in the magazine *Die Horen*, it was introduced within a series of stories by the figure of an elderly clergyman who said that he was going to tell a fairy story that would remind them of "everything and nothing." And so it is. Goethe's Fairy Tale will surely speak to those who are able to hear, and say nothing to those who can't.

The last words should now rest with Goethe and his inspired creation, *The Fairy Tale of The Green Snake and the Beautiful Lily*. Early in the Fairy Tale the Gold King asks the Green Snake:

"What is more noble than Gold?"
"Light," replies the Snake.
"And what is more refreshing than Light?" asks the King.
"Speech," replies the Snake.

Author's footnote: I make no claims to originality, but record a debt of gratitude to those who have devoted study, research and no little insight into Goethe's life and his creative work of the Fairy Tale. In particular, Paul Marshall Allen and Joan Deris Allen.

Tom Raines is the editor of New View *magazine, in which this article first appeared in 2003.*

Bibliography
The Time is at Hand! Paul Marshall Allen and Joan Deris Allen, 1995, Anthoposophic Press.
The Wholeness of Nature - Goethe's Way of Science, Henri Bortoft, 1996, Floris Books.
Selected works of Rudolf Steiner.

The Fairy Tale of
the Green Snake and
the Beautiful Lily

Johann Wolfgang von Goethe

Translated by Thomas Carlyle

This text is reproduced in style from the translation first published in Prater's Magnum in 1832, and again when it was included in Thomas Carlyle's Collected Works.

In his little Hut, by the great River, which a heavy rain had swoln to overflowing, lay the ancient Ferryman, asleep, wearied by the toil of the day. In the middle of the night, loud voices awoke him; he heard that it was travellers wishing to be carried over.

Stepping out, he saw two large Will-o'-wisps, hovering to and fro on his boat, which lay moored: they said, they were in violent haste, and should have been already on the other side. The old Ferryman made no loitering; pushed off, and steered with his usual skill obliquely through the stream; while the two strangers whiffled and hissed together, in an unknown very rapid tongue, and every now and then broke out in loud laughter, hopping about, at one time on the gunwale and the seats, at another on the bottom of the boat.

The boat is heeling!" cried the old man; "if you don't be quiet, it will overset; be seated, gentlemen of the wisp!"

At this advice they burst into a fit of laughter, mocked the old man, and were more unquiet than ever. He bore their mischief with patience, and soon reached the farther shore.

"Here is for your labour!" cried the travellers; and as they shook themselves, a heap of glittering gold-pieces jingled down into the wet boat. "For Heaven's sake, what are you about?" cried the old man; "you will ruin me forever! Had a single piece of gold got into the water, the stream, which cannot suffer gold, would have risen in horrid waves, and swallowed both my skiff and me; and who knows how it might have fared with you in that case? Here, take back your gold."

"We can take nothing back, which we have once shaken from us," said the Lights.

"Then you give me the trouble," said the old man, stooping down, and gathering the pieces into his cap, "of raking them together, and carrying them ashore and burying them."

The Lights had leaped from the boat, but the old man cried: "Stay; where is my fare?"

"If you take no gold, you may work for nothing," cried the Will-o'-wisps. — "You must know that I am only to be paid with fruits of the earth." — "Fruits of the earth? we despise them, and have never tasted them." — "And yet I cannot let you go, till you have promised that you will deliver me three Cabbages, three Artichokes, and three large Onions."

The Lights were making-off with jests; but they felt themselves, in some inexplicable manner, fastened to the ground: it was the unpleasantest feeling they had ever had. They engaged to pay him his demand as soon as possible: he let them go, and pushed away. He was gone a good distance, when they called to him: "Old man! Holla, old man! The main point is forgotten!" He was off, however, and did not hear them. He had fallen quietly down that side of the River, where, in a rocky spot, which the water never reached, he meant to bury the pernicious gold. Here, between two high crags, he found a monstrous chasm; shook the metal into it, and steered back to his cottage.

Now in this chasm lay the fair green Snake, who was roused from her sleep by the gold coming chinking down. No sooner did she fix her eye on the glittering coins, than she ate them all up, with the greatest relish, on the spot; and carefully picked out such pieces as were scattered in the chinks of the rock.

Scarcely had she swallowed them, when, with extreme delight, she began to feel the metal melting in her inwards, and spreading all over her body; and soon, to her lively joy, she

I Midnight.
"The Time is at Hand"

observed that she was grown transparent and luminous. Long ago she had been told that this was possible; but now being doubtful whether such a light could last, her curiosity and the desire to be secure against the future, drove her from her cell, that she might see who it was that had shaken-in this precious metal. She found no one. The more delightful was it to admire her own appearance, and her graceful brightness, as she crawled along through roots and bushes, and spread out her light among the grass. Every leaf seemed of emerald, every flower was dyed with new glory. It was in vain that she crossed the solitary thickets; but her hopes rose high, when, on reaching the open country, she perceived from afar a brilliancy resembling her own. "Shall I find my like at last, then?" cried she, and hastened to the spot. The toil of crawling through bog and reeds gave her little thought; for though she liked best to live in dry grassy spots of the mountains, among the clefts of rocks, and for most part fed on spicy herbs, and slaked her thirst with mild dew and fresh spring-water, yet for the sake of this dear gold, and in the hope of this glorious light, she would have undertaken anything you could propose to her.

At last, with much fatigue, she reached a wet rushy spot in the swamp, where our two Will-o'-wisps were frisking to and fro. She shoved herself along to them; saluted them, was happy to meet such pleasant gentlemen related to her family. The Lights glided towards her, skipped up over her, and laughed in their fashion. "Lady Cousin," said they, "you are of the horizontal line, yet what of that? It is true we are related only by the look; for, observe you," here both the Flames, compressing their whole breadth, made themselves as high and peaked as possible, "how prettily this taper length beseems us gentlemen of the vertical line! Take it not amiss of us, good Lady; what family can boast of such a thing? Since there ever was a Jack-o'-lantern in the world, no one of them has either sat or lain."

The Snake felt exceedingly uncomfortable in the company of these relations; for, let her hold her head as high as possible, she found that she must bend it to the earth again, would she stir from the spot; and if in the dark thicket she had been extremely satisfied with her appearance, her splendor in the presence of these cousins seemed to lessen every moment, nay she was afraid that at last it would go out entirely.

In this embarrassment she hastily asked: If the gentlemen could not inform her, whence the glittering gold came, that had fallen a short while ago into the cleft of the rock; her own opinion was, that it had been a golden shower, and had trickled down direct from the sky. The Will-o'-wisps laughed, and shook themselves, and a multitude of gold-pieces came clinking down about them. The Snake pushed nimbly forwards to eat the coin. "Much good may it do you, Mistress," said the dapper gentlemen: "we can help you to a little more." They shook themselves again several times with great quickness, so that the Snake could scarcely gulp the precious victuals fast enough. Her splendor visibly began increasing; she was really shining beautifully, while the Lights had in the meantime grown rather lean and short of stature, without however in the smallest losing their good-humor.

"I am obliged to you forever," said the Snake, having got her wind again after the repast; "ask of me what you will; all that I can I will do."

"Very good!" cried the Lights. "Then tell us where the fair Lily dwells? Lead us to the fair Lily's palace and garden; and do not lose a moment, we are dying of impatience to fall down at her feet."

"This service," said the Snake with a deep sigh, "I cannot now do for you. The fair Lily dwells, alas, on the other side of the water."—"Other side of the water? And we have come across it, this stormy night! How cruel is the River to divide us! Would it not be possible to call the old man back?"

"It would be useless," said the Snake; "for if you found him ready on the bank, he would not take you in; he can carry anyone to this side, none to yonder."

"Here is a pretty kettle of fish!" cried the Lights: "are there no other means of getting through the water?" — "There are other means, but not at this moment. I myself could take you over, gentlemen, but not till noon." — "That is an hour we do not like to travel in." — "Then you may go across in the evening, on the great Giant's shadow." — "How is that?" — "The great Giant lives not far from this; with his body he has no power; his hands cannot lift a straw, his shoulders could not bear a faggot of twigs; but with his shadow he has power over much, nay all. At sunrise and sunset therefore he is strongest; so at evening you merely put yourself upon the back of his shadow, the Giant walks softly to the bank, and the shadow carries you across the water. But if you please, about the hour of noon, to be in waiting at that corner of the wood where the bushes overhang the bank, I myself will take you over and present you to the fair Lily: or on the other hand, if you dislike the noontide, you have just to go at nightfall to that bend of the rocks, and pay a visit to the Giant; he will certainly receive you like a gentleman."

With a slight bow, the Flames went off; and the Snake at bottom was not discontented to get rid of them; partly that she might enjoy the brightness of her own light, partly satisfy a curiosity with which, for a long time, she had been agitated in a singular way.

In the chasm, where she often crawled hither and thither, she had made a strange discovery. For although in creeping up and down this abyss, she had never had a ray of light, she could well enough discriminate the objects in it, by her sense of touch. Generally she met with nothing but irregular productions of Nature; at one time she would wind between the teeth of large crystals, at another she would feel the barbs and hairs of native silver, and now and then carry out with her to the light some straggling jewels. But to her no small wonder, in a rock which was closed on every side, she had come on certain objects which betrayed the shaping hand of man. Smooth walls on which she could not climb, sharp regular corners, well-formed pillars; and what seemed strangest of all, human figures which she had entwined more than once, and which appeared to her to be of brass, or of the finest polished marble. All these experiences she now wished to combine by the sense of sight, thereby to confirm what as yet she only guessed. She believed she could illuminate the whole of that subterranean vault by her own light; and hoped to get acquainted with these curious things at once. She hastened back; and soon found, by the usual way, the cleft by which she used to penetrate the Sanctuary.

On reaching the place, she gazed around with eager curiosity; and though her shining could not enlighten every object in the rotunda, yet those nearest her were plain enough. With astonishment and reverence she looked up into a glancing niche, where the image of an august King stood formed of pure Gold. In size the figure was beyond the stature of man, but by its shape it seemed the likeness of a little rather than a tall person. His handsome body was encircled with an unadorned mantle; and a garland of oak bound his hair together.

No sooner had the Snake beheld this reverend figure, than the King began to speak, and asked: "Whence comest thou?" — "From the chasms where the gold dwells," said the

Snake. — "What is grander than gold?" inquired the King. — "Light," replied the Snake. — "What is more refreshing than light?" said he. — "Speech," answered she.

During this conversation, she had squinted to a side, and in the nearest niche perceived another glorious image. It was a Silver King in a sitting posture; his shape was long and rather languid; he was covered with a decorated robe; crown, girdle and sceptre were adorned with precious stones: the cheerfulness of pride was in his countenance; he seemed about to speak, when a vein which ran dimly-colored over the marble wall, on a sudden became bright, and diffused a cheerful light throughout the whole Temple. By this brilliancy the Snake perceived a third King, made of Brass, and sitting mighty in shape, leaning on his club, adorned with a laurel garland, and more like a rock than a man. She was looking for the fourth, which was standing at the greatest distance from her; but the wall opened, while the glittering vein started and split, as lightning does, and disappeared.

A Man of middle stature, entering through the cleft, attracted the attention of the Snake. He was dressed like a peasant, and carried in his hand a little Lamp, on whose still flame you liked to look, and which in a strange manner, without casting any shadow, enlightened the whole dome.

"Why comest thou, since we have light?" said the golden King.—"You know that I may not enlighten what is dark." — "Will my Kingdom end?" said the silver King. — "Late or never," said the old Man.

With a stronger voice the brazen King began to ask: "When shall I arise?"—"Soon," replied the Man. — "With whom shall I combine?" said the King. — "With thy elder brothers," said the Man. — "What will the youngest do?" inquired the King. — "He will sit down," replied the Man.

"I am not tired," cried the fourth King, with a rough faltering voice.

While this speech was going on, the Snake had glided softly round the Temple, viewing everything; she was now looking at the fourth King close by him. He stood leaning on a pillar; his considerable form was heavy rather than beautiful. But what metal it was made of could not be determined. Closely inspected, it seemed a mixture of the three metals which its brothers had been formed of. But in the founding, these materials did not seem to have combined together fully; gold and silver veins ran irregularly through a brazen mass, and gave the figure an unpleasant aspect.

Meanwhile the gold King was asking of the Man, "How many secrets knowest thou?" — "Three," replied the Man. — "Which is the most important?" said the silver King. — "The open one," replied the other. — "Wilt thou open it to us also?" said the brass King. — "When I know the fourth," replied the Man. — "What care I?" grumbled the composite King, in an undertone.

"I know the fourth," said the Snake; approached the old Man, and hissed somewhat in his ear. "The time is at hand!" cried the old Man, with a strong voice. The temple reëchoed, the metal statues sounded; and that instant the old Man sank away to the westward, and the Snake to the eastward; and both of them passed through the clefts of the rock, with the greatest speed.

All the passages, through which the old Man travelled, filled themselves, immediately behind him, with gold; for his Lamp had the strange property of changing stone into gold, wood

II. Morning

into silver, dead animals into precious stones, and of annihilating all metals. But to display this power, it must shine alone. If another light were beside it, the Lamp only cast from it a pure clear brightness, and all living things were refreshed by it.

Picture II   Morning

The old Man entered his cottage, which was built on the slope of the hill. He found his Wife in extreme distress. She was sitting at the fire weeping, and refusing to be consoled. "How unhappy am I!" cried she: "Did not I entreat thee not to go away tonight?" — "What is the matter, then?" inquired the husband, quite composed.

"Scarcely wert thou gone," said she, sobbing, "when there came two noisy Travellers to the door: unthinkingly I let them in; they seemed be a couple of genteel, very honorable people; they were dressed in flames, you would have taken them for Will-o'-wisps. But no sooner were they in the house, than they began, like impudent varlets, to compliment me, and grew so forward that I feel ashamed to think of it."

"No doubt," said the husband with a smile, "the gentlemen were jesting: considering thy age, they might have held by general politeness."

"Age! What age?" cried the Wife: "wilt thou always be talking of my age? How old am I, then? — General politeness! But I know what I know. Look round there what a face the walls have; look at the old stones, which I have not seen these hundred years; every film of gold have they licked away, thou couldst not think how fast; and still they kept assuring me that it tasted far beyond common gold. Once they had swept the walls, the fellows seemed to be in high spirits, and truly in that little while they had grown much broader and brighter. They now began to be impertinent again, they patted me, and called me their queen, they shook themselves, and a shower of gold-pieces sprang from them; see how they are shining there under the bench! But ah, what misery! Poor Mops ate a coin or two; and look, he is lying in the chimney, dead. Poor Pug. O well-a-day! I did not see it till they were gone; else I had never promised to pay the Ferryman the debt they owe him." —"What do they owe him?" said the Man. — "Three Cabbages," replied the Wife, "three Artichokes and three Onions: I engaged to go when it was day, and take them to the River."

"Thou mayest do them that civility," said the old Man; "they may chance to be of use to us again."

"Whether they will be of use to us I know not; but they promised and vowed that they would."

Meantime the fire on the hearth had burnt low; the old Man covered-up the embers with a heap of ashes, and put the glittering gold-pieces aside; so that his little Lamp now gleamed alone, in the fairest brightness. The walls again coated themselves with gold, and Mops changed into the prettiest onyx that could be imagined. The alternation of the brown and black in this precious stone made it the most curious piece of workmanship.

"Take thy basket," said the Man, "and put the onyx into it; then take the three Cabbages, the three Artichokes and the three Onions; place them round little Mops, and carry them to the River. At noon the Snake will take thee over; visit the fair Lily, give her the onyx, she will make it alive by her touch, as by her touch she kills whatever is alive already. She will

28

have a true companion in the little dog. Tell her, not to mourn; her deliverance is near; the greatest misfortune she may look upon as the greatest happiness; for the time is at hand."

The old Woman filled her basket, and set out as soon as it was day. The rising sun shone clear from the other side of the River, which was glittering in the distance; the old Woman walked with slow steps, for the basket pressed upon her head, and it was not the onyx that so burdened her. Whatever lifeless thing she might be carrying, she did not feel the weight of it; on the other hand, in those cases the basket rose aloft, and hovered along above her head. But to carry any fresh herbage, or any little living animal, she found exceedingly laborious. She had travelled on for some time, in a sullen humor, when she halted suddenly in fright, for she had almost trod upon the Giant's shadow, which was stretching towards her across the plain. And now, lifting up her eyes, she saw the monster of a Giant himself, who had been bathing in the River, and was just come out, and she knew not how she should avoid him. The moment he perceived her, he began saluting her in sport, and the hands of his shadow soon caught hold of the basket. With dexterous ease they picked away from it a Cabbage, an Artichoke and an Onion, and brought them to the Giant's mouth, who then went his way up the River, and let the Woman go in peace.

Picture III Noon

She considered whether it would not be better to return, and supply from her garden the pieces she had lost; and amid these doubts, she still kept walking on, so that in a little while she was at the bank of the River. She sat long waiting for the Ferryman, whom she perceived at last, steering over with a very singular traveller. A young, noble-looking, handsome man, whom she could not gaze upon enough, slept out of the boat.

"What is it you bring?" cried the old Man. — "The greens which those two Will-o'-wisps owe you," said the Woman, pointing to her ware. As the Ferryman found only two of each sort, he grew angry, and declared he would have none of them. The Woman earnestly entreated him to take them; told him that she could not now go home, and that her burden for the way which still remained was very heavy. He stood by his refusal, and assured her that it did not rest with him. "What belongs to me," said he, "I must leave lying nine hours in a heap, touching none of it, till I have given the River its third." After much higgling, the old Man at last replied: "There is still another way. If you like to pledge yourself to the River, and declare yourself its debtor, I will take the six pieces; but there is some risk in it." — "If I keep my word, I shall run no risk?" — "Not the smallest. Put your hand into the stream," continued he, "and promise that within four-and-twenty hours you will pay the debt."

The old Woman did so; but what was her affright, when on drawing out her hand, she found it black as coal! She loudly scolded the old Ferryman; declared that her hands had always been the fairest part of her; that in spite of her hard work, she had all along contrived to keep these noble members white and dainty. She looked at the hand with indignation, and exclaimed in a despairing tone: "Worse and worse! Look, it is vanishing entirely; it is grown far smaller than the other."

"For the present it but seems so," said the old Man; "if you do not keep your word, however, it may prove so in earnest. The hand will gradually diminish, and at length disappear

29

altogether, though you have the use of it as formerly. Everything as usual you will be able to perform with it, only nobody will see it." — "I had rather that I could not use it, and no one could observe the want," cried she: "but what of that, I will keep my word, and rid myself of this black skin, and all anxieties about it." Thereupon she hastily took up her basket, which mounted of itself over her head, and hovered free above her in the air, as she hurried after the Youth, who was walking softly and thoughtfully down the bank. His noble form and strange dress had made a deep impression on her.

His breast was covered with a glittering coat of mail; in whose wavings might be traced every motion of his fair body. From his shoulders hung a purple cloak; around his uncovered head flowed abundant brown hair in beautiful locks: his graceful face, and his well-formed feet were exposed to the scorching of the sun. With bare soles, he walked composedly over the hot sand; and a deep inward sorrow seemed to blunt him against all external things.

The garrulous old Woman tried to lead him into conversation; but with his short answers he gave her small encouragement or information; so that in the end, notwithstanding the beauty of his eyes, she grew tired of speaking with him to no purpose, and took leave of him with these words: "You walk too slow for me, worthy sir; I must not lose a moment, for I have to pass the River on the green Snake, and carry this fine present from my husband to the fair Lily." So saying she stept faster forward; but the fair Youth pushed on with equal speed, and hastened to keep up with her. "You are going to the fair Lily!" cried he; "then our roads are the same. But what present is this you are bringing her?"

"Sir," said the Woman, "it is hardly fair, after so briefly dismissing the questions I put to you, to inquire with such vivacity about my secrets. But if you like to barter, and tell me your adventures, I will not conceal from you how it stands with me and my presents." They soon made a bargain: the dame disclosed her circumstances to him; told the history of the Pug, and let him see the singular gift.

He lifted this natural curiosity from the basket, and took Mops, who seemed as if sleeping softly, into his arms. "Happy beast!" cried he; "thou wilt be touched by her hands, thou wilt be made alive by her; while the living are obliged to fly from her presence to escape a mournful doom. Yet why say I mournful? Is it not far sadder and more frightful to be injured by her look, than it would be to die by her hand? Behold me," said he to the Woman; "at my years, what a miserable fate have I to undergo! This mail which I have honorably borne in war, this purple which I sought to merit by a wise reign, Destiny has left me; the one as a useless burden, the other as an empty ornament. Crown, and sceptre, and sword are gone; and I am as bare and needy as any other son of earth; for so unblessed are her bright eyes, that they take from every living creature they look-on all its force, and those whom the touch of her hand does not kill are changed to the state of shadows wandering alive.

Thus did he continue to bewail, nowise contenting the old Woman's curiosity, who wished for information not so much of his internal as of his external situation. She learned neither the name of his father, nor of his kingdom. He stroked the hard Mops, whom the sunbeams and the bosom of the youth had warmed as if he had been living. He inquired narrowly about the Man with the Lamp, about the influences of the sacred light, appearing to expect much good from it in his melancholy case.

Amid such conversation, they descried from afar the majestic arch of the Bridge, which

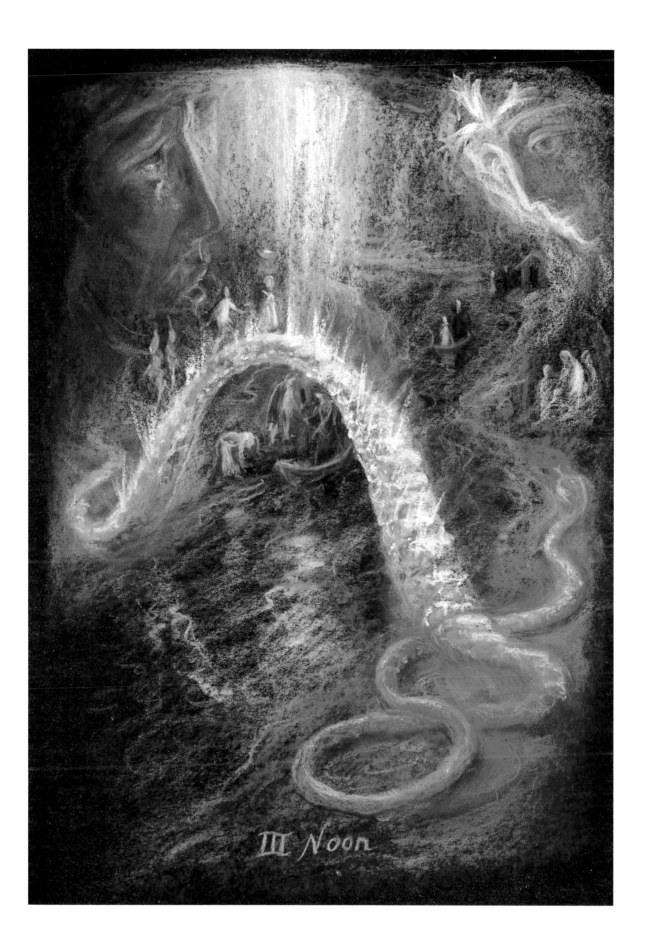

III Noon

extended from the one bank to the other, glittering with the strangest colors in the splendors of the sun. Both were astonished; for until now they had never seen this edifice so grand. "Howl" cried the Prince, "was it not beautiful enough, as it stood before our eyes, piled out of jasper and agate? Shall we not fear to tread it, now that it appears combined, in graceful complexity of emerald and chrysopras and chrysolite?" Neither of them knew the alteration that had taken place upon the Snake: for it was indeed the Snake, who every day at noon curved herself over the River, and stood forth in the form of a bold-swelling bridge. The travellers stept upon it with a reverential feeling, and passed over it in silence.

No sooner had they reached the other shore, than the bridge began to heave and stir; in a little while, it touched the surface of the water, and the green Snake in her proper form came gliding after the wanderers. They had scarcely thanked her for the privilege of crossing on her back, when they found that, besides them three, there must be other persons in the company, whom their eyes could not discern. They heard a hissing, which the Snake also answered with a hissing; they listened, and at length caught what follows: "We shall first look about us in the fair Lily's Park," said a pair of alternating voices; "and then request you at nightfall, so soon as we are anywise presentable, to introduce us to this paragon of beauty. At the shore of the great Lake you will find us." — "Be it so," replied the Snake; and a hissing sound died away in the air.

Picture IV   Twilight

Our three travellers now consulted in what order they should introduce themselves to the fair Lady; for however many people might be in her company, they were obliged to enter and depart singly, under pain of suffering very hard severities.

The Woman with the metamorphosed Pug in the basket first approached the garden, looking round for her Patroness; who was not difficult to find, being just engaged in singing to her harp. The finest tones proceeded from her first like circles on the surface of the still lake, then like a light breath they set the grass and the bushes in motion. In a green enclosure, under the shadow of a stately group of many diverse trees, was she seated; and again did she enchant the eyes, the ears and the heart of the Woman, who approached with rapture, and swore within herself that since she saw her last, the fair one had grown fairer than ever. With eager gladness, from a distance, she expressed her reverence and admiration for the lovely maiden. "What a happiness to see you! What a Heaven does your presence spread around you! How charmingly the harp is leaning on your bosom, how softly your arms surround it, how it seems as if longing to be near you, and how it sounds so meekly under the touch of your slim fingers! Thrice-happy youth, to whom it were permitted to be there!"

So speaking she approached; the fair Lily raised her eyes; let her hands drop from the harp, and answered: "Trouble me not with untimely praise; I feel my misery but the more deeply. Look here, at my feet lies the poor Canary-bird, which used so beautifully to accompany my singing; it would sit upon my harp, and was trained not to touch me; but today, while I, refreshed by sleep, was raising a peaceful morning hymn, and my little singer was pouring forth his harmonious tones more gaily than ever, a Hawk darts over my head; the poor little creature, in affright, takes refuge in my bosom, and I feel the last palpitations of its

IV Twilight

departing life. The plundering Hawk indeed was caught by my look, and fluttered fainting down into the water; but what can his punishment avail me? my darling is dead, and his grave will but increase the mournful bushes of my garden."

"Take courage, fairest Lily!" cried the Woman, wiping off a tear, which the story of the hapless maiden had called into her eyes; "compose yourself; my old man bids me tell you to moderate your lamenting, to look upon the greatest misfortune as a forerunner of the greatest happiness, for the time is at hand; and truly," continued she, "the world is going strangely on of late. Do but look at my hand, how black it is! As I live and breathe, it is grown far smaller: I must hasten, before it vanish altogether! Why did I engage to do the Will-o'-wisps a service, why did I meet the Giant's shadow, and dip my hand in the River? Could you not afford me a single cabbage, an artichoke and an onion? I would give them to the River, and my hand were white as ever, so that I could almost show it with one of yours."

"Cabbages and onions thou mayest still find; but artichokes thou wilt search for in vain. No plant in my garden bears either flowers or fruit; but every twig that I break, and plant upon the grave of a favorite, grows green straightway, and shoots up in fair boughs. All these groups, these bushes, these groves my hard destiny has so raised around me. These pines stretching out like parasols, these obelisks of cypresses, these colossal oaks and beeches, were all little twigs planted by my hand, as mournful memorials in a soil that otherwise is barren."

To this speech the old Woman had paid little heed; she was looking at her hand, which, in presence of the fair Lily, seemed every moment growing blacker and smaller. She was about to snatch her basket and hasten off, when she noticed that the best part of her errand had been forgotten. She lifted out the onyx Pug, and set him down, not far from the fair one, in the grass. "My husband," said she, "sends you this memorial; you know that you can make a jewel live by touching it. This pretty faithful dog will certainly afford you much enjoyment; and my grief at losing him is brightened only by the thought that he will be in your possession."

The fair Lily viewed the dainty creature with a pleased and, as it seemed, with an astonished look. "Many signs combine," said she, "that breathe some hope into me: but ah! Is it not a natural deception which makes us fancy, when misfortunes crowd upon us, that a better day is near?

"What can these many signs avail me?
My Singer's Death, thy coal-black Hand?
This Dog of Onyx, that can never fail me?
And coming at the Lamp's command?

From human joys removed forever,
With sorrows compassed round I sit:
Is there a Temple at the River?
Is there a Bridge? Alas, not yet!"

The good old dame had listened with impatience to this singing, which the fair Lily accompanied with her harp, in a way that would have charmed any other. She was on the point of taking leave, when the arrival of the green Snake again detained her. The Snake had caught the last lines of the song, and on this matter forthwith began to speak comfort to the fair Lily.

"The prophecy of the Bridge is fulfilled!" cried the Snake: "you may ask this worthy dame how royally the arch looks now. What formerly was untransparent jasper, or agate, allowing but a gleam of light to pass about its edges, is now become transparent precious stone. No beryl is so clear, no emerald so beautiful of hue."

"I wish you joy of it," said Lily; "but you will pardon me if I regard the prophecy as yet unaccomplished. The lofty arch of your bridge can still but admit foot-passengers; and it is promised us that horses and carriages and travellers of every sort shall, at the same moment, cross this bridge in both directions. Is there not something said, too, about pillars, which are to arise of themselves from the waters of the River?"

The old Woman still kept her eyes fixed on her hand; she here interrupted their dialogue, and was taking leave. "Wait a moment," said the fair Lily, "and carry my little bird with you. Bid the Lamp change it into topaz; I will enliven it by my touch; with your good Mops it shall form my dearest pastime: but hasten, hasten; for, at sunset, intolerable putrefaction will fasten on the hapless bird, and tear asunder the fair combination of its form forever."

The old Woman laid the little corpse, wrapped in soft leaves, into her basket, and hastened away.

"However it may be," said the Snake, recommencing their interrupted dialogue, "the Temple is built."

"But it is not at the River," said the fair one.

"It is yet resting in the depths of the Earth," said the Snake; "I have seen the Kings and conversed with them."

"But when will they arise?" inquired Lily.

The Snake replied: "I heard resounding in the Temple these deep words, *The time is at hand.*"

A pleasing cheerfulness spread over the fair Lily's face: "'Tis the second time," said she, "that I have heard these happy words today: when will the day come for me to hear them thrice?"

She arose, and immediately there came a lovely maiden from the grove, and took away her harp. Another followed her, and folded-up the fine carved ivory stool, on which the fair one had been sitting, and put the silvery cushion under her arm. A third then made her appearance, with a large parasol worked with pearls; and looked whether Lily would require her in walking. These three maidens were beyond expression beautiful; and yet their beauty but exalted that of Lily, for it was plain to every one that they could never be compared to her.

Meanwhile the fair one had been looking, with a satisfied aspect, at the strange onyx Mops. She bent down and touched him, and that instant he started up. Gaily he looked around, ran hither and thither, and at last, in his kindest manner, hastened to salute his bene-factress. She took him in her arms, and pressed him to her. "Cold as thou art," cried she, "and though but a half-life works in thee, thou art welcome to me; tenderly will I love thee, prettily will I play with thee, softly caress thee, and firmly press thee to my bosom." She then let him go, chased him from her, called him back, and played so daintily with him, and ran about so gaily and so innocently with him on the grass, that with new rapture you viewed and partici-pated in her joy, as a little while ago her sorrow had attuned every heart to sympathy.

This cheerfulness, these graceful sports were interrupted by the entrance of the woeful Youth. He stepped forward, in his former guise and aspect; save that the heat of the day appeared to have fatigued him still more, and in the presence of his mistress he grew paler every moment. He bore upon his hand a Hawk, which was sitting quiet as a dove, with its body shrunk, and its wings drooping.

"It is not kind in thee," cried Lily to him, "to bring that hateful thing before my eyes, the monster, which today has killed my little singer."

"Blame not the unhappy bird!" replied the Youth; "rather blame thyself and thy destiny; and leave me to keep beside me the companion of my woe."

Meanwhile Mops ceased not teasing the fair Lily; and she replied to her transparent favourite, with friendly gestures. She clapped her hands to scare him off; then ran, to entice him after her. She tried to get him when he fled, and she chased him away when he attempted to press near her. The Youth looked on in silence, with increasing anger; but at last, when she took the odious beast, which seemed to him unutterably ugly, on her arm, pressed it to her white bosom, and kissed its black snout with her heavenly lips, his patience altogether failed him, and full of desperation he exclaimed: "Must I, who by a baleful fate exist beside thee, perhaps to the end, in an absent presence; who by thee have lost my all, my very self; must I see before my eyes, that so unnatural a monster can charm thee into gladness, can awaken thy attachment, and enjoy thy embrace? Shall I any longer keep wandering to and fro, measuring my dreary course to that side of the River and to this? No, there is still a spark of the old heroic spirit sleeping in my bosom; let it start this instant into its expiring flame! If stones may rest in thy bosom, let me be changed to stone; if thy touch kills, I will die by thy hands."

So saying he made a violent movement; the Hawk flew from his finger, but he himself rushed towards the fair one; she held out her hands to keep him off, and touched him only the sooner. Consciousness forsook him; and she felt with horror the beloved burden lying on her bosom. With a shriek she started back, and the gentle Youth sank lifeless from her arms upon the ground.

The misery had happened! The sweet Lily stood motionless gazing on the corpse. Her heart seemed to pause in her bosom; and her eyes were without tears. In vain did Mops try to gain from her any kindly gesture; with her friend, the world for her was all dead as the grave. Her silent despair did not look round for help; she knew not of any help.

On the other hand, the Snake bestirred herself the more actively; she seemed to meditate deliverance; and in fact her strange movements served at least to keep away, for a little, the immediate consequences of the mischief. With her limber body, she formed a wide circle round the corpse, and seizing the end of her tail between her teeth, she lay quite still.

Picture V   Midnight

Ere long one of Lily's fair waiting-maids appeared; brought the ivory folding-stool, and with friendly beckoning constrained her mistress to sit down on it. Soon afterwards there came a second; she had in her hand a fire-coloured veil, with which she rather decorated than concealed the fair Lily's head. The third handed her the harp, and scarcely had she drawn the gorgeous instrument towards her, and struck some tones from its strings, when the first maid returned with a clear round mirror; took her station opposite the fair one; caught her looks in

V Midnight

the glass, and threw back to her the loveliest image that was to be found in Nature. Sorrow heightened her beauty, the veil her charms, the harp her grace; and deeply as you wished to see her mournful situation altered, not less deeply did you wish to keep her image, as she now looked, forever present with you.

With a still look at the mirror, she touched the harp; now melting tones proceeded from the strings, now her pain seemed to mount, and the music in strong notes responded to her woe; sometimes she opened her lips to sing, but her voice failed her; and ere long her sorrow melted into tears, two maidens caught her helpfully in their arms, the harp sank from her bosom, scarcely could the quick servant snatch the instrument and carry it aside.

"Who gets us the Man with the Lamp, before the Sun set?" hissed the Snake, faintly, but audibly: the maids looked at one another, and Lily's tears fell faster. At this moment came the Woman with the Basket, panting and altogether breathless. "I am lost, and maimed for life!" cried she; "see how my hand is almost vanished; neither Ferryman nor Giant would take me over, because I am the River's debtor; in vain did I promise hundreds of cabbages and hundreds of onions; they will take no more than three; and no artichoke is now to be found in all this quarter."

"Forget your own care," said the Snake, "and try to bring help here; perhaps it may come to yourself also. Haste with your utmost speed to seek the Will-o'-wisps; it is too light for you to see them, but perhaps you will hear them laughing and hopping to and fro. If they be speedy, they may cross upon the Giant's shadow, and seek the Man with the Lamp, and send him to us."

The Woman hurried off at her quickest pace, and the Snake seemed expecting as impatiently as Lily the return of the Flames. Alas! The beam of the sinking Sun was already gliding only the highest summits of the trees in the thicket, and long shadows were stretching over lake and meadow; the Snake hitched up and down impatiently, and Lily dissolved in tears.

In this extreme need, the Snake kept looking round on all sides; for she was afraid every moment that the Sun would set, and corruption penetrate the magic circle, and the fair youth immediately moulder away. At last she noticed sailing high in the air, with purple-red feathers, the Prince's Hawk, whose breast was catching the last beams of the Sun. She shook herself for joy at this good omen; nor was she deceived; for shortly afterwards the Man with the Lamp was seen gliding towards them across the Lake, fast and smoothly, as if he had been travelling on skates.

The Snake did not change her posture; but Lily rose and called to him: "What good spirit sends thee, at the moment when we were desiring thee, and needing thee, so much?"

"The spirit of my Lamp," replied the Man, "has impelled me, and the Hawk has conducted me. My Lamp sparkles when I am needed, and I just look about me in the sky for a signal; some bird or meteor points to the quarter towards which I am to turn. Be calm, fairest Maiden! Whether I can help, I know not; an individual helps not, but he who combines himself with many at the proper hour. We will postpone the evil, and keep hoping. Hold thy circle fast," continued he, turning to the Snake; then set himself upon a hillock beside her, and illuminated the dead body. "Bring the little Bird hither too, and lay it in the circle!" The maidens took the little corpse from the basket, which the old Woman had left standing, and did as he directed.

Meanwhile the Sun had set; and as the darkness increased, not only the Snake and the old Man's Lamp began shining in their fashion, but also Lily's veil gave-out a soft light, which gracefully tinged, as with a meek dawning red, her pale cheeks and her white robe. The party looked at one another, silently reflecting; care and sorrow were mitigated by a sure hope.

It was no unpleasing entrance, therefore, that the Woman made, attended by the two gay Flames, which in truth appeared to have been very lavish in the interim, for they had again become extremely meagre; yet they only bore themselves the more prettily for that, towards Lily and the other ladies. With great tact and expressiveness, they said a multitude of rather common things to these fair persons; and declared themselves particularly ravished by the charm which the gleaming veil spread over Lily and her attendants. The ladies modestly cast down their eyes, and the praise of their beauty made them really beautiful. All were peaceful and calm, except the old Woman. In spite of the assurance of her husband, that her hand could diminish no farther, while the Lamp shone on it, she asserted more than once, that if things went on thus, before midnight this noble member would have utterly vanished.

The Man with the Lamp had listened attentively to the conversation of the Lights; and was gratified that Lily had been cheered, in some measure, and amused by it. And, in truth, midnight had arrived they knew not how. The old Man looked to the stars, and then began speaking: "We are assembled at the propitious hour; let each perform his task, let each do his duty; and a universal happiness will swallow-up our individual sorrows, as a universal grief consumes individual joys."

At these words arose a wondrous hubbub; for all the persons in the party spoke aloud, each for himself, declaring what they had to do; only the three maids were silent; one of them had fallen asleep beside the harp, another near the parasol, the third by the stool; and you could not blame them much, for it was late. The Fiery Youths, after some passing compliments which they devoted to the waiting-maids, had turned their sole attention to the Princess, as alone worthy of exclusive homage.

"Take the mirror," said the Man to the Hawk; "and with the first sunbeam illuminate the three sleepers, and awake them, with light reflected from above."

The Snake now began to move; she loosened her circle, and rolled slowly, in large rings, forward to the River. The two Will-o'-wisps followed with a solemn air: you would have taken them for the most serious Flames in Nature. The old Woman and her husband seized the Basket, whose mild light they had scarcely observed till now; they lifted it at both sides, and it grew still larger and more luminous; they lifted the body of the Youth into it, laying the Canary-bird upon his breast; the Basket rose into the air and hovered above the old Woman's head, and she followed the Will-o'-wisps on foot. The fair Lily took Mops on her arm, and followed the Woman; the Man with the Lamp concluded the procession; and the scene was curiously illuminated by these many lights.

But it was with no small wonder that the party saw, when they approached the River, a glorious arch mount over it, by which the helpful Snake was affording them a glittering path. If by day they had admired the beautiful transparent precious stones, of which the Bridge seemed formed; by night they were astonished at its gleaming brilliancy. On the upper side the clear circle marked itself sharp against the dark sky, but below, vivid beams were darting to the centre, and exhibiting the airy firmness of the edifice. The procession slowly moved across it; and the Ferryman, who saw it from his hut afar off, considered with astonishment the gleaming circle, and the strange lights which were passing over it.

No sooner had they reached the other shore, than the arch began, in its usual way, to swag up and down, and with a wavy motion to approach the water. The Snake then came on land, the Basket placed itself upon the ground, and the Snake again drew her circle round it. The old Man stooped towards her, and said: "What hast thou resolved on?"

"To sacrifice myself rather than be sacrificed," replied the Snake; "promise me that thou wilt leave no stone on shore."

The old Man promised; then addressing Lily: "Touch the Snake," said he, "with thy left hand, and thy lover with thy right." Lily knelt, and touched the Snake and the Prince's body. The latter in the instant seemed to come to life; he moved in the Basket, nay he raised himself into a sitting posture; Lily was about to clasp him; but the old Man held her back, and himself assisted the Youth to rise, and led him forth from the Basket and the circle.

The Prince was standing; the Canary-bird was fluttering on his shoulder; there was life again in both of them, but the spirit had not yet returned; the fair Youth's eyes were open, yet he did not see, at least he seemed to look on all without participation. Scarcely had their admiration of this incident a little calmed, when they observed how strangely it had fared in the meanwhile with the Snake. Her fair taper body had crumbled into thousands and thousands of shining jewels: the old Woman reaching at her Basket had chanced to come against the circle; and of the shape or structure of the Snake there was now nothing to be seen, only a bright ring of luminous jewels was lying in the grass.

The old Man forthwith set himself to gather the stones into the Basket; a task in which his wife assisted him. They next carried the Basket to an elevated point on the bank; and here the man threw its whole lading, not without contradiction from the fair one and his wife, who would gladly have retained some part of it, down into the River. Like gleaming twinkling stars the stones floated down with the waves; and you could not say whether they lost themselves in the distance, or sank to the bottom.

"Gentlemen," said he with the Lamp, in a respectful tone to the Lights, "I will now show you the way, and open you the passage; but you will do us an essential service, if you please to unbolt the door, by which the Sanctuary must be entered at present, and which none but you can unfasten."

The Lights made a stately bow of assent, and kept their place. The old Man of the Lamp went foremost into the rock, which opened at his presence; the Youth followed him, as if mechanically; silent and uncertain, Lily kept at some distance from him; the old Woman would not be left, and stretched-out her hand, that the light of her husband's Lamp might still fall upon it. The rear was closed by the two Will-o'-wisps, who bent the peaks of their flames towards one another, and appeared to be engaged in conversation.

They had not gone far till the procession halted in front of a large brazen door, the leaves of which were bolted with a golden lock. The Man now called upon the Lights to advance; who required small entreaty, and with their pointed flames soon ate both bar and lock.

The brass gave a loud clang, as the doors sprang suddenly asunder; and the stately figures of the Kings appeared within the Sanctuary, illuminated by the entering Lights.

All bowed before these dread sovereigns, especially the Flames made a profusion of the daintiest reverences.

After a pause, the gold King asked: "Whence come ye?" — "From the world," said the old Man. — "Whither go ye?" said the silver King. "Into the world," replied the Man. — "What would ye with us?" cried the brazen King. "Accompany you," replied the Man.

The composite King was about to speak, when the gold one addressed the Lights, who had got too near him: "Take yourselves away from me, my metal was not made for you." Thereupon they turned to the silver King, and clasped themselves about him; and his robe glittered beautifully in their yellow brightness. "You are welcome," said he, "but I cannot feed you; satisfy yourselves elsewhere, and bring me your light." They removed; and gliding past the brazen King, who did not seem to notice them, they fixed on the compounded King. "Who will govern the world?" cried he, with a broken voice. "He who stands upon his feet," replied the old Man. — "I am he," said the mixed King. "We shall see," replied the Man; "for the time is at hand."

Picture VI   Morning

The fair Lily fell upon the old Man's neck, and kissed him cordially. "Holy Sage!" cried she, "a thousand times I thank thee; for I hear that fateful word the third time." She had scarcely spoken, when she clasped the old Man still faster; for the ground began to move beneath them; the Youth and the old Woman also held by one another; the Lights alone did not regard it.

You could feel plainly that the whole temple was in motion; as a ship that softly glides away from the harbour, when her anchors are lifted; the depths of the Earth seemed to open for the Building as it went along. It struck on nothing; no rock came in its way.

For a few instants, a small rain seemed to drizzle from the opening of the dome; the old Man held the fair Lily fast, and said to her: "We are now beneath the River; we shall soon be at the mark." Ere long they thought the Temple made a halt; but they were in an error; it was mounting upwards.

And now a strange uproar rose above their heads. Planks and beams in disordered combination now came pressing and crashing in at the opening of the dome. Lily and the Woman started to a side; the Man with the Lamp laid hold of the Youth, and kept standing still. The little cottage of the Ferryman, — for it was this which the Temple in ascending had severed from the ground and carried up with it, — sank gradually down, and covered the old Man and the Youth.

The women screamed aloud, and the Temple shook, like a ship running unexpectedly aground. In sorrowful perplexity, the Princess and her old attendant wandered round the cottage in the dawn; the door was bolted, and to their knocking no one answered. They knocked more loudly, and were not a little struck, when at length the wood began to ring. By virtue of the Lamp locked up in it, the hut had been converted from the inside to the outside into solid silver. Ere long too its form changed; for the noble metal shook aside the accidental shape of planks, posts and beams, and stretched itself out into a noble case of beaten ornamented workmanship. Thus a fair little temple stood erected in the middle of the large one; or if you will, an Altar worthy of the Temple.

By a staircase which ascended from within, the noble Youth now mounted aloft, lighted by the old Man with the Lamp; and, as it seemed, supported by another, who advanced in a white short robe, with a silver rudder in his hand; and was soon recognized as the Ferryman, the former possessor of the cottage.

The fair Lily mounted the outer steps, which led from the floor of the Temple to the Altar; but she was still obliged to keep herself apart from her Lover. The old Woman, whose hand in the absence of the Lamp had grown still smaller, cried: "Am I, then, to be unhappy after all? Among so many miracles, can there be nothing done to save my hand?" Her husband pointed to the open door, and said to her: "See, the day is breaking; haste, bathe thyself in the River." — "What an advice!" cried she; "it will make me all black; it will make me vanish altogether; for my debt is not yet paid." — "Go," said the Man, "and do as I advise thee; all debts are now paid."

The old Woman hastened away; and at that moment appeared the rising Sun, upon the rim of the dome. The old Man stept between the Virgin and the Youth, and cried with a loud voice: "There are three which have rule on Earth; Wisdom, Appearance and Strength." At the first word, the gold King rose; at the second, the silver one; and at the third, the brass King slowly rose, while the mixed King on a sudden very awkwardly plumped down.

Whoever noticed him could scarcely keep from laughing, solemn as the moment was; for he was not sitting, he was not lying, he was not leaning, but shapelessly sunk together.

The Lights, who till now had been employed upon him, drew to a side; they appeared, although pale in the morning radiance, yet once more well-fed, and in good burning condition; with their peaked tongues, they had dexterously licked-out the gold veins of the colossal figure to its very heart. The irregular vacuities which this occasioned had continued empty for a time, and the figure had maintained its standing posture. But when at last the very tenderest filaments were eaten out, the image crashed suddenly together; and that, alas, in the very parts which continue unaltered when one sits down; whereas the limbs, which should have bent, sprawled themselves out unbowed and stiff. Whoever *could* not laugh was obliged to turn away his eyes; this miserable shape and no-shape was offensive to behold.

The Man with the Lamp now led the handsome Youth, who still kept gazing vacantly before him, down from the Altar, and straight to the brazen King. At the feet of this mighty Potentate lay a sword in a brazen sheath. The young man girt it round him. "The sword on the left, the right free!" cried the brazen voice. They next proceeded to the silver King; he bent his sceptre to the Youth; the latter seized it with his left hand, and the King in a pleasing voice said: "Feed the sheep!" On turning to the golden King, he stooped with gestures of paternal blessing, and pressing his oaken garland on the young man's head, said: "Understand what is highest!"

During this progress, the old Man had carefully observed the Prince. After girding-on the sword, his breast swelled, his arms waved, and his feet trod firmer; when he took the sceptre in his hand, his strength appeared to soften, and by an unspeakable charm to become still more subduing; but as the oaken garland came to deck his hair, his features kindled, his eyes gleamed with inexpressible spirit, and the first word of his mouth was "Lily!"

"Dearest Lily!" cried he, hastening up the silver stairs to her, for she had viewed his

VI Morning

progress from the pinnacle of the Altar; "Dearest Lily! What more precious can a man, equipped with all, desire for himself than innocence and the still affection which thy bosom brings me? O my friend!" continued he, turning to the old Man, and looking at the three statues; "glorious and secure is the kingdom of our fathers; but thou hast forgotten the fourth power, which rules the world, earlier, more universally, more certainly, the power of Love." With these words, he fell upon the lovely maiden's neck; she had cast away her veil, and her cheeks were tinged with the fairest, most imperishable red.

Here the old Man said with a smile: "Love does not rule; but it trains, and that is more."

Picture VII   Bright Noonday

Amid this solemnity, this happiness and rapture, no one had observed that it was now broad day; and all at once, on looking through the open portal, a crowd of altogether unexpected objects met the eye. A large space surrounded with pillars formed the fore-court, at the end of which was seen a broad and stately Bridge stretching with many arches across the River. It was furnished, on both sides, with commodious and magnificent colonnades for foot-travellers, many thousands of whom were already there, busily passing this way or that. The broad pavement in the centre was thronged with herds and mules, with horsemen and carriages, flowing like two streams, on their several sides, and neither interrupting the other. All admired the splendor and convenience of the structure; and the new King and his Spouse were delighted with the motion and activity of this great people, as they were already happy in their own mutual love.

"Remember the Snake in honor," said the Man with the Lamp; "thou owest her thy life; thy people owe her the Bridge, by which these neighboring banks are now animated and combined into one land. Those swimming and shining jewels, the remains of her sacrificed body, are the piers of this royal bridge; upon these she has built and will maintain herself."

The party were about to ask some explanation of this strange mystery, when there entered four lovely maidens at the portal of the Temple. By the Harp, the Parasol, and the Folding-stool, it was not difficult to recognize the waiting-maids of Lily; but the fourth, more beautiful than any of the rest, was an unknown fair one, and in sisterly sportfulness she hastened with them through the Temple, and mounted the steps of the Altar.

"Wilt thou have better trust in me another time, good wife?" said the Man with the Lamp to the fair one: "Well for thee, and every living thing that bathes this morning in the River!"

The renewed and beautified old Woman, of whose former shape no trace remained, embraced with young eager arms the Man with the Lamp, who kindly received her caresses. "If I am too old for thee," said he, smiling, "thou mayest choose another husband today; from this hour no marriage is of force, which is not contracted anew."

"Dost thou not know, then," answered she, "that thou too art grown younger?" — "It delights me if to thy young eyes I seem a handsome youth: I take thy hand anew, and am well content to live with thee another thousand years."

The Queen welcomed her new friend, and went down with her into the interior of the Altar, while the King stood between his two men, looking towards the Bridge, and attentively

VII Bright Noonday

contemplating the busy tumult of the people.

But his satisfaction did not last; for ere long he saw an object which excited his displeasure. The great Giant, who appeared not yet to have awoke completely from his morning sleep, came stumbling along the Bridge, producing great confusion all around him. As usual, he had risen stupefied with sleep, and had meant to bathe in the well-known bay of the River; instead of which he found firm land, and plunged upon the broad pavement of the Bridge. Yet although he reeled into the midst of men and cattle in the clumsiest way, his presence, wondered at by all, was felt by none; but as the sunshine came into his eyes, and he raised his hands to rub them, the shadows of his monstrous fists moved to and fro behind him with such force and awkwardness, that men and beasts were heaped together in great masses, were hurt by such rude contact, and in danger of being pitched into the River.

The King, as he saw this mischief, grasped with an involuntary movement at his sword; but he bethought himself, and looked calmly at his sceptre, then at the Lamp and the Rudder of his attendants. "I guess thy thoughts," said the Man with the Lamp; "but we and our gifts are powerless against this powerless monster. Be calm! He is doing hurt for the last time, and happily his shadow is not turned to us."

Meanwhile the Giant was approaching nearer; in astonishment at what he saw with open eyes, he had dropt his hands; he was now doing no injury, and came staring and agape into the fore-court.

He was walking straight to the door of the Temple, when all at once in the middle of the court, he halted, and was fixed to the ground. He stood there like a strong colossal statue, of reddish glittering stone, and his shadow pointed out the hours, which were marked in a circle on the floor around him, not in numbers, but in noble and expressive emblems.

Much delighted was the King to see the monster's shadow turned to some useful purpose; much astonished was the Queen, who, on mounting from within the Altar, decked in royal pomp, with her virgins, first noticed the huge figure, which almost closed the prospect from the Temple to the Bridge.

Meanwhile the people had crowded after the Giant, as he ceased to move; they were walking round him, wondering at his metamorphosis. From him they turned to the Temple, which they now first appeared to notice, and pressed towards the door.

At this instant the Hawk with the mirror soared aloft above the dome; caught the light of the Sun, and reflected it upon the group, which was standing on the Altar. The King, the Queen, and their attendants, in the dusky concave of the Temple, seemed illuminated by a heavenly splendor, and the people fell upon their faces. When the crowd had recovered and risen, the King with his followers had descended into the Altar, to proceed by secret passages into his palace; and the multitude dispersed about the Temple to content their curiosity. The three Kings that were standing erect they viewed with astonishment and reverence; but the more eager were they to discover what mass it could be that was hid behind the hangings, in the fourth niche; for by some hand or another, charitable decency had spread over the resting-place of the fallen King a gorgeous curtain, which no eye can penetrate, and no hand may dare to draw aside.

The people would have found no end to their gazing and their admiration, and the crowding multitude would have even suffocated one another in the Temple, had not their attention been again attracted to the open space.

Unexpectedly some gold-pieces, as if falling from the air, came tinkling down upon the marble flags; the nearest passers-by rushed thither to pick them up; the wonder was repeated several times, now here, now there. It is easy to conceive that the shower proceeded from our two retiring Flames, who wished to have a little sport here once more, and were thus gaily spending, ere they went away, the gold which they had licked from the members of the sunken King. The people still ran eagerly about, pressing and pulling one another, even when the gold had ceased to fall. At length they gradually dispersed, and went their way; and to the present hour the Bridge is swarming with travellers, and the Temple is the most frequented on the whole Earth.

Other work by David Newbatt
published by Wynstones Press

Wynstones Press publishes and distributes a range of Books, Cards, Prints and Advent Calendars from a variety of artists and authors. Included amongst these is a range of work by David Newbatt, including:

PARZIVAL The Quest for the Holy Grail

Illustrated by David Newbatt.

Parzival is one of the great classic stories of the last millennium, a colourful tale from the time of knighthood, full of romance, love and adventure. David Newbatt's illustrations in this book bring a refreshingly vivid and direct interpretation of the Quest for the Holy Grail. The accompanying text gives a brief introduction to some of the many characters and events portrayed in this epic tale, in a clear and concise way. Parzival is a great story for reading by the fireside. It is also a deep and intense piece of literature in which is portrayed an individual's archetypal biography, which can speak to us today in our own search for the modern Grail Temple.

240 pages with 112 colour illustrations. Size 210 x 297 mm. Hardbound.

TWELVE ASPECTS OF MICHAEL Contrasted by their Counter-images

Written by Christoph-Andreas Lindenberg and illustrated by David Newbatt.

This book explores images of St Michael in such a way to reveal a twelve-fold balance of key noble qualities that the human being can strive for, together with, in contrast, the all too recognisable failings of human nature, as revealed in their counter-images.

48 pages with 12 colour illustrations. Size 210 x 297 mm. Hardbound.

CARDS

Wynstones Press publishes a wide range of both folded cards and postcards reproduced from work by David Newbatt. These include a selection of landscapes,religious and other themes. Also available are sets of cards illustrating a variety of work including: Goethe's Fairy Tale of the Green Snake and the Beautiful Lily; Twelve Aspects of Michael; Parzival and the Norwegian tale of Olaf Åsteson.

For further details on the above please contact:

Wynstones Press

Ruskin Glass Centre, Wollaston Road, Stourbridge, West Midlands DY8 4HE. England.
www.wynstonespress.com